Introducing FANNY

Stories and Pictures by
KATE SPOHN

Orchard Books   New York

Orchard Books, A division of Franklin Watts, Inc.
387 Park Avenue South, New York, NY 10016

Manufactured in the United States of America.
Printed by General Offset Company, Inc.
Bound by Horowitz/Rae. Book design by Mina Greenstein.
The text of this book is set in 18 pt. Janson.
The illustrations are colored pencil.
10 9 8 7 6 5 4 3 2 1

Library of Congress Cataloging-in-Publication Data
Spohn, Kate. Introducing Fanny / story and pictures by Kate Spohn.
p. cm. Summary: Relates the adventures of Fanny, a pear, and her friend
Margarita, a banana.
ISBN 0-531-05920-0 ISBN 0-531-08520-1 (lib.)
[1. Pear—Fiction. 2. Banana—Fiction. 3. Friendship—Fiction.] I. Title.
PZ7.S7636In 1991 [E]—dc20 90-7736 CIP AC

To Ruth Farnsworth,
who has taught me more
than the Irish jig

Fanny and Margarita

Today Fanny hates the way she looks.
Her mother and little sister Annabell say she looks pretty.
But Fanny wants to be tall and slender
like her best friend Margarita.
Fanny tries on everything in her wardrobe,
thinking something will do the trick.

But nothing will change the fact that she is a pear,
plump and green, and not a banana,
slender and yellow.

So Fanny puts on what she wore yesterday,
and she and her friend Margarita jump rocks and skip stones
in the river.

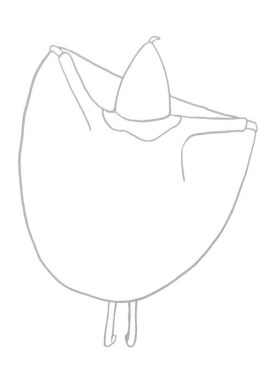

Fanny's Handiwork

Fanny is going to make a doll for Annabell's birthday.
She wants special buttons, so she and Margarita
go to buy them.
They choose five pink oval buttons,
three brown leaf-shaped buttons,
and two green crescent buttons.

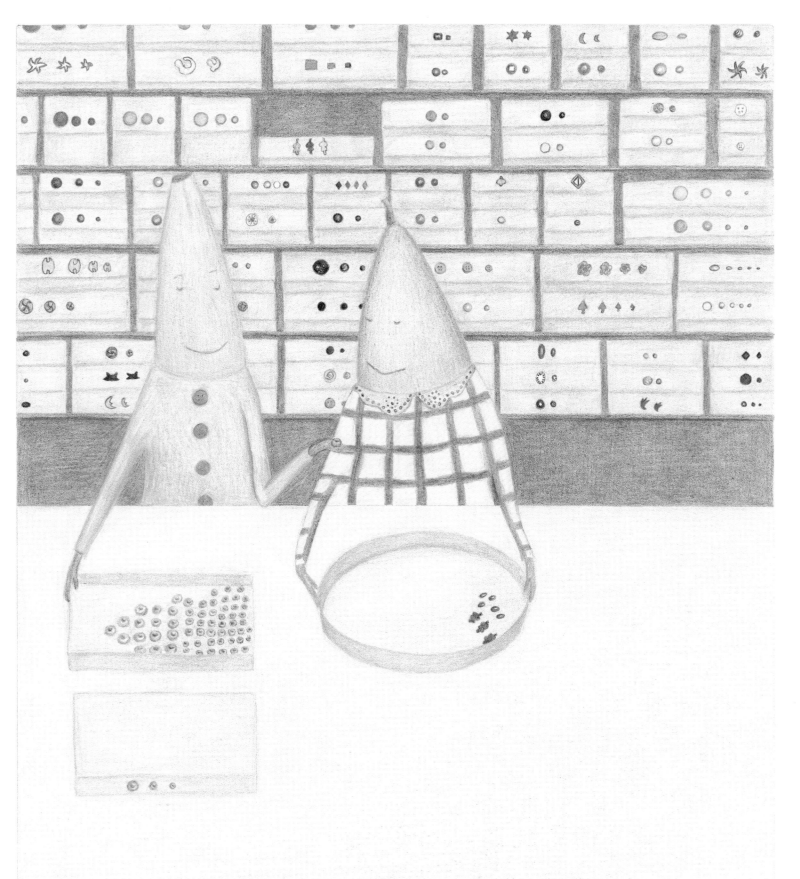

Margarita watches as Fanny sets to work.

First Fanny cuts the doll's body out of green flannel,

sews up the sides, turns it inside out,

stuffs it with rags, and sews up the top.

Next she sews a snip of brown yarn

to the top of the doll's head,

sews on green crescent buttons for eyes,

and stitches a mouth.

Then Fanny sews a dress adorned with buttons

and a pink felt collar.

"Now *this* is a doll!" exclaims Margarita.

Annabell thinks so too. It becomes her favorite doll.

Fanny's Thoughts

Fanny is a good thinker in the bathroom.
She runs the hot and cold water, pours in bubble bath,
and when there is a full blanket of bubbles,
steps into the tub.

Fanny lies back in the tub and thinks.
She thinks of her friend Margarita.
She thinks of her mother's friend Harriet
who is soon coming to visit.
She thinks of mermaids.
And she thinks of doughnuts.

Fanny uses soap, and scrubs from the top of her head
to the bottom of her feet.
She rinses and wonders whether there are doughnut shops
for mermaids, and if so,
do they have jelly-filled, her favorite?

Later, when she and Fanny are eating doughnuts together,
Margarita is amazed, wondering whether mermaids have doughnuts.

Harriet Arrives

Fanny and Annabell are glad to see
their mother's best friend, Harriet.
After dinner the four of them sing in rounds.
"You have a beautiful voice," Harriet tells Fanny.
Then, when it is late,
Fanny goes upstairs for her favorite pillow,
her own stuffed doll, and her pajamas.
She says good-night to her bedroom and all her things,
and comes downstairs to sleep.

Fanny lies thinking of Annabell having a very nice sleep
in her own bed.
She thinks of Harriet sleeping above in *her* bed.
Fanny tosses and turns, missing her bed, her blanket,
her treasures all around . . . and then she is asleep.

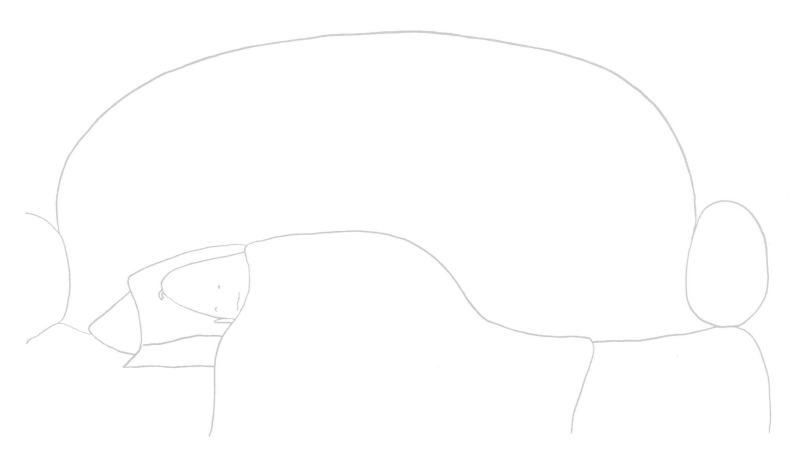

In the morning, Harriet thanks Fanny for the use of her bed.
She teaches the girls the Irish jig before leaving.
Fanny does a happy jig because tonight
she will sleep in her own bed, and tomorrow
she can teach the Irish jig to Margarita . . .

. . . which she does.
da da
da da
da da da da da da da da
da da
da da
da da da da da da da da!

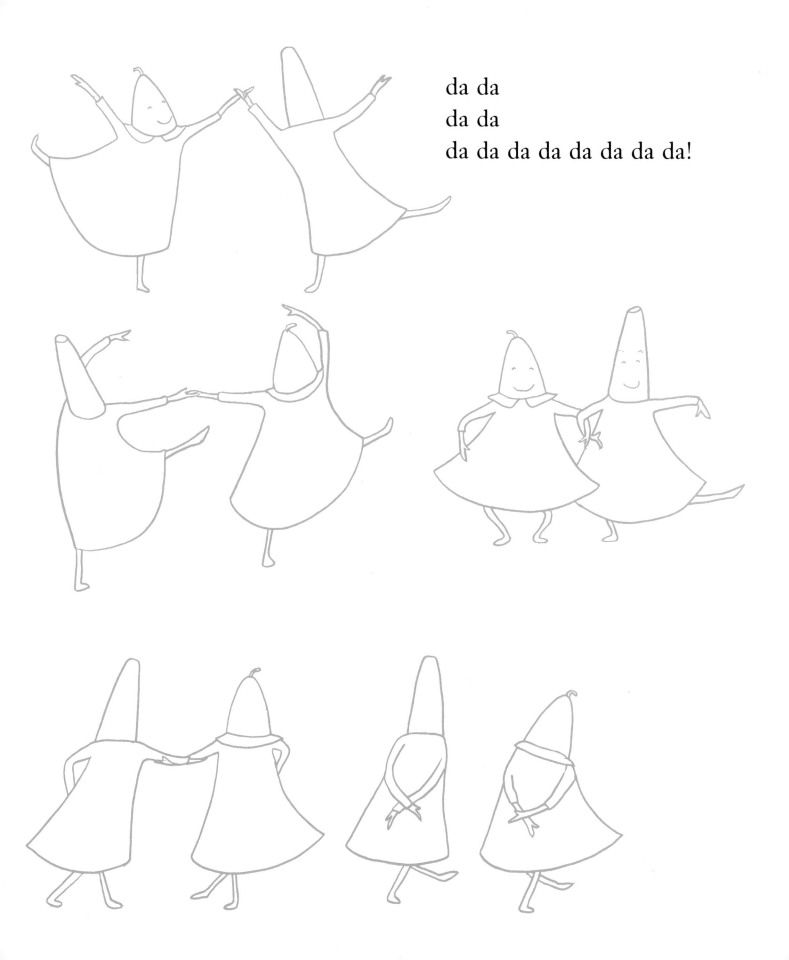

da da
da da
da da da da da da da da!